The Pet Shop

ALLAN AHLBERG • ANDRÉ AMSTUTZ

PUFFIN

In a dark dark – Woof! – street there is a dark dark – Woof! – house. Behind the dark dark – Woof! – house there is a dark dark – Woof! – garden. In the dark dark – Woof! – garden there is a very dark dark – Woof! – hole

. . . and a little noisy dog – Woof!

One night, the big skeleton
and the little skeleton
go into the garden.
"I'm fed up with this dog,"
says the little skeleton.
"Me too," says the big skeleton.
"All he does is dig holes – and bark."
"Woof!" barks the dog.

"I know," says the little skeleton,
"let's go to the pet shop –
and swap him."
"Good idea!" the big skeleton says.
"Howl!" howls the dog.

So off they – Woof! – go,
out of the dark dark garden,
down the dark dark street
and into the dark dark – Miaow! –
– Squeak! – Grunt! – pet shop.
The big skeleton and the little skeleton
swap the dog – Woof! – skeleton

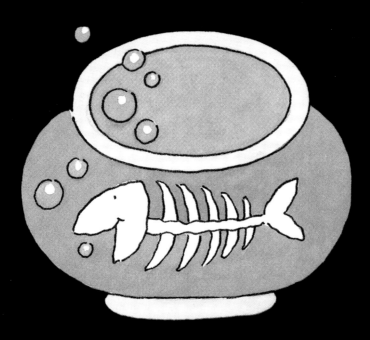

. . . for a goldfish.

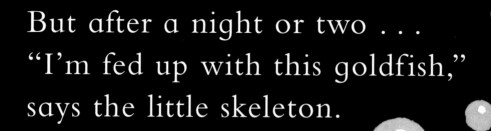

But after a night or two . . .
"I'm fed up with this goldfish,"
says the little skeleton.

"Me too," says the big skeleton.
"All it does is blow bubbles –
and swim."

So off they go again,
out of the dark dark house,
down the dark dark street
and back to the dark dark – Miaow! –
– Snort! – Croak! – pet shop.
The big skeleton and the little skeleton
swap the goldfish – Bubble, bubble! – skeleton
. . . for a parrot.

But after another night or two . . .
"I'm fed up with this parrot,"
says the little skeleton.
"Me too," says the big skeleton.
"All he does is shout rude names."
"Big bum!" shouts the parrot.

So off they go again,
back to the dark dark – Miaow! –
– Big bum! – pet shop.
The big skeleton and the little skeleton
swap the parrot skeleton

. . . for a hippopotamus.
But the hippopotamus
is no good either.
All he does . . .

. . . is fill the room!

So – Wobble, wobble! –
back they go again
and swap the hippopotamus
. . . for a rabbit.

And after a night or two . . .
"I love this rabbit,"
says the little skeleton.
"Me too," says the big skeleton.
"He's not big,
he's not cheeky
and he doesn't blow bubbles."

The only trouble is – *he* is not a *he*.

So after a few more nights . . .
"I'm fed up with these rabbits,"
says the little skeleton.
"And these!" the big skeleton says.

Back they go to the pet shop.
"And I'm fed up with this
– Miaow! – Moo! – Baa! –
pet shop as well!"
says the little skeleton.

The pet-shop skeleton
puts the rabbits in a hutch.
"Cheer up!" he says.
"I've got just the thing for you."

He gives them a big box
with little holes in it.
"But don't open it until
you get home."

After that the big skeleton
and the little skeleton
leave the dark dark –
Miaow! – pet shop, and
hurry down the dark dark street
to the dark dark house
. . . and the dark dark cellar.

They put the box on the table.
"I wonder what it is,"
says the little skeleton.
"Me too," says the big skeleton.
. . . "WOOF!" barks the box.

The End

PUFFIN BOOKS

Published by the Penguin Group
Penguin Books Ltd, 80 Strand, London WC2R 0RL, England
Penguin Group (USA), Inc., 375 Hudson Street, New York, New York 10014, USA
Penguin Books Australia Ltd, 250 Camberwell Road, Camberwell, Victoria 3124, Australia
Penguin Books Canada Ltd, 10 Alcorn Avenue, Toronto, Ontario, Canada M4V 3B2
Penguin Books India (P) Ltd, 11 Community Centre, Panchsheel Park, New Delhi 110 017, India
Penguin Group (NZ), cnr Airborne and Rosedale Roads, Albany, Auckland 1310, New Zealand
Penguin Books (South Africa) (Pty) Ltd, 24 Sturdee Avenue, Rosebank 2196, South Africa

Penguin Books Ltd, Registered Offices: 80 Strand, London WC2R 0RL, England

www.penguin.com

First published by William Heinemann Ltd 1990
First published in Puffin Books 2004
This edition published 2005
1 3 5 7 9 10 8 6 4 2

Text copyright © Allan Ahlberg, 1990
Illustrations copyright © André Amstutz, 1990
All rights reserved

The moral right of the author and illustrator has been asserted

Set in Bembo

Manufactured in China

British Library Cataloguing in Publication Data
A CIP catalogue record for this book is available from the British Library

ISBN 0-141-50045-X